Jellyfish Hugs is book 1 in
the Below H₂O Book Series

Written by: Bessie Schenk

below H₂O
sea-mingly simple tales for kids

Colophon

Jellyfish Hugs ©
A Below H2O Series Book ©
A Division of Happy Forward BV

Copyright © by Bessie Schenk
Text & Illustrations: DTP-hulp.nl
Formatting: DTP-hulp.nl
Author & Illustrator photos by:
Paco van Leeuwen Photography

First Print: May, 2024
ISBN: 9789083414409

NUR: 273
Published in the Netherlands
First printed in Poland
Series trademark in progress

All rights reserved, including the reproduction in whole or in any part in any form. No part of this publication may be reproduced, stored in automated databases, or made public, in any form or by any means, electronic, mechanical, by photocopying, recording or any other means, without prior notice or written permission from the publisher, Bessie Schenk of Happy Forward BV.

Jellyfish Hugs

Story:
Bessie Schenk

Illustrations:
Mireille van Yperen

Dedicated to Arya, Roberto, Adrienne.

Also, to my Dad, Han. Who reminds me each day that being kind is always the most worthwhile endeavor.

Please don't misunderstand. It's just hard for us to trust long enough to get close to you. This is especially challenging for me.

See, here's the thing - I just cannot stand to see someone sad. Like, ever. The problem is that when someone is sad, I have this benevolent and uncontrollable urge to sigh, wait for it,

HUG!

This might not seem to be a big issue for you who are reading this because you've probably got those magical things called arms. But, for me, I have all these tentacles. And to make matters worse, I have two extra long rogue ones.

Bet you didn't even notice because without you realizing it, they've already snuck off the page and have begun wrapping around you in a big slimy squeeze.

I've tried tying them in a bow. Nope.

I've tried painting them to blend in with the ocean floor. Nope.

I've even tried putting shoes on them to distract people and make them think I'm a crab. Nope.

For the record, crabs don't exactly have the best gig either.

But for me the issue is that the minute someone cries or feels sad, these two extra long wigglers seem to have a mind of their own.

And today is Monday, which means it's a school day. Sigh. BIG sigh. I tried getting out of going by pretending to have a bad case of sea legs, but my Dad didn't buy it.

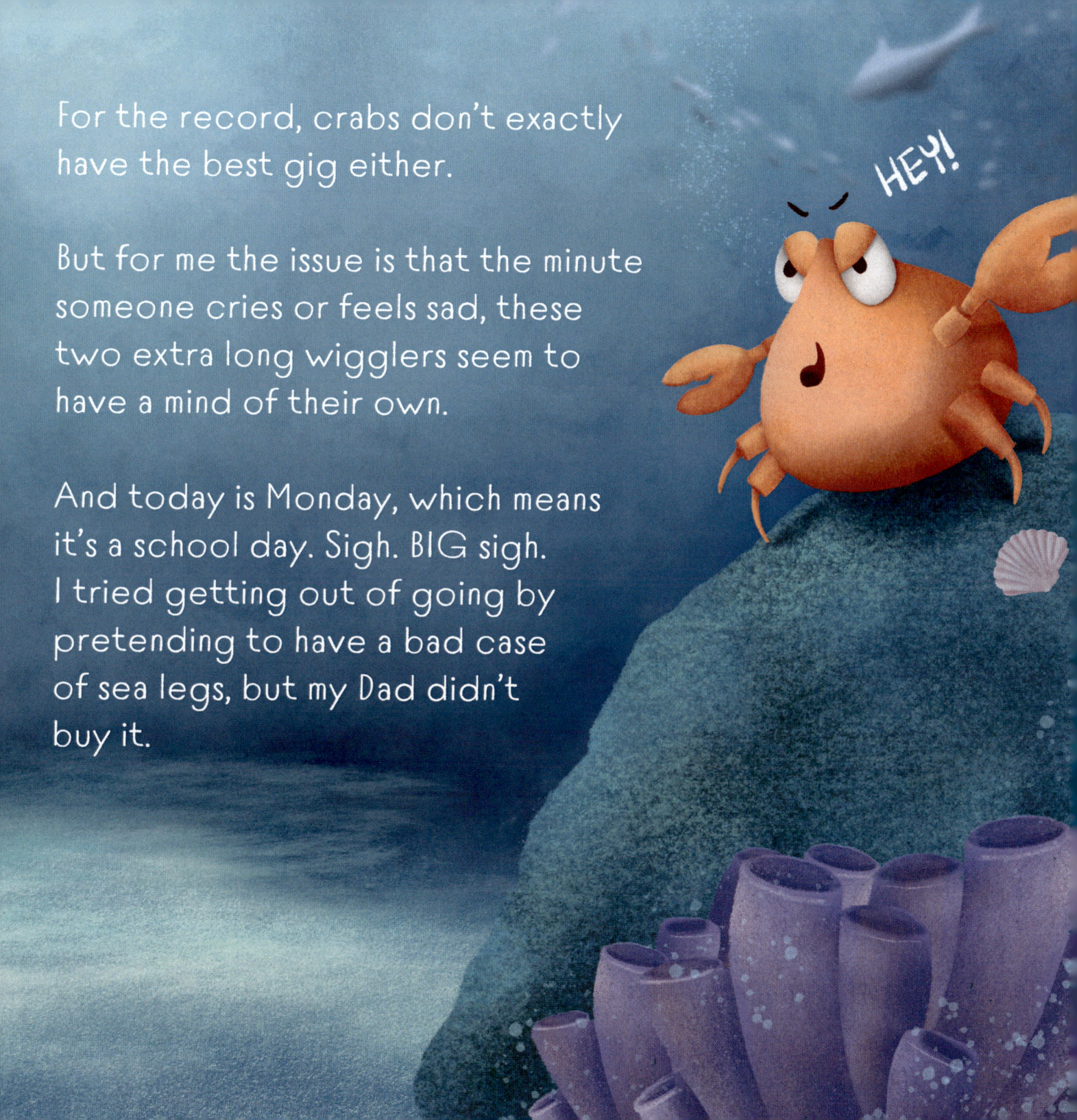

HEY!

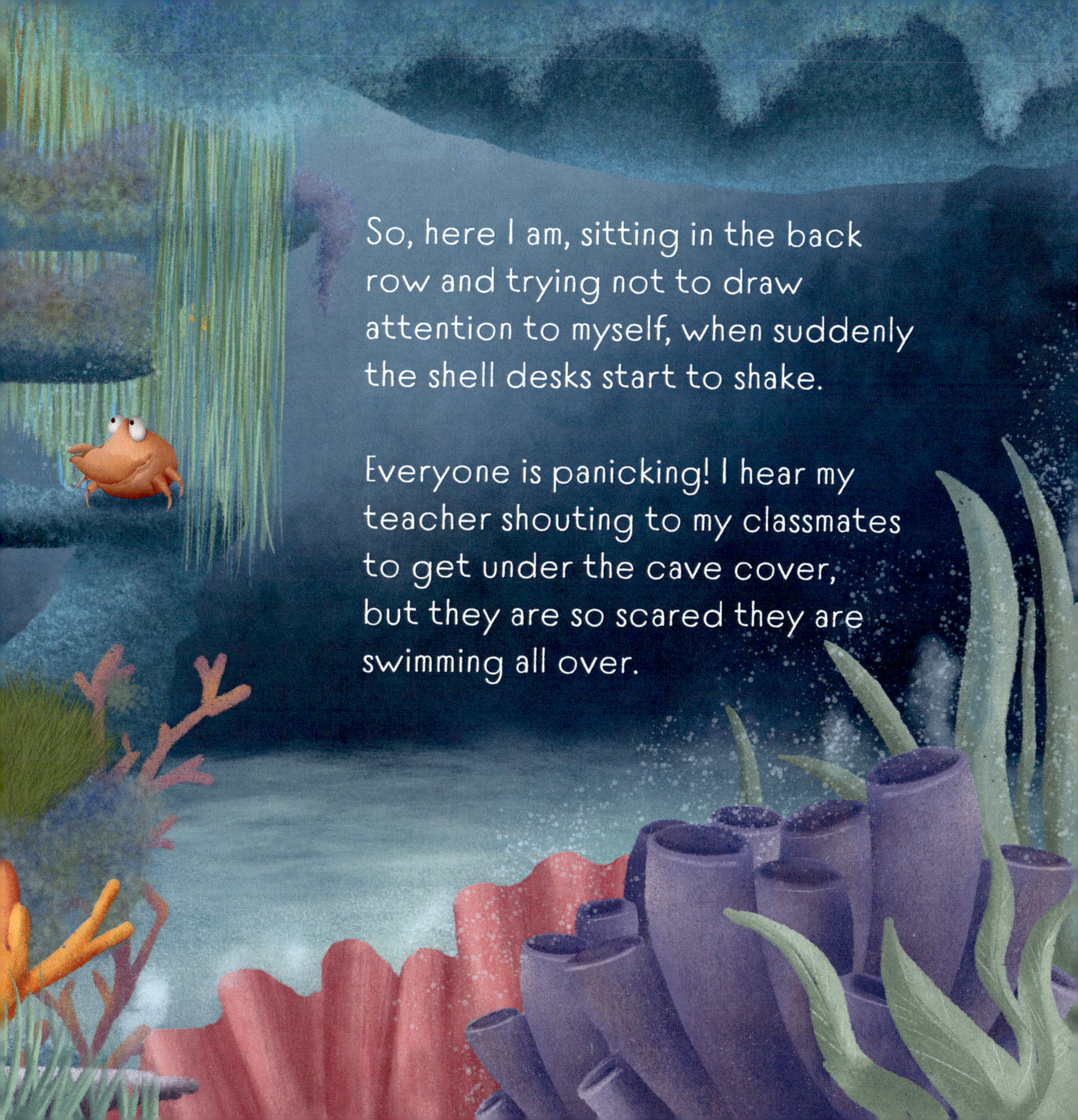

So, here I am, sitting in the back row and trying not to draw attention to myself, when suddenly the shell desks start to shake.

Everyone is panicking! I hear my teacher shouting to my classmates to get under the cave cover, but they are so scared they are swimming all over.

They have stretched way out, and one by one have gathered all my classmates - even the blowfish (who at this moment is having some serious floatation issues) into a gargantuan HUG!

Now, it seems all my mates are still scared, but slowly and steadily, my super duper master hug has pulled us all under the cave cover.

After what feels like forever, the shaking stops. Then, the dust starts to settle. I can see the clam board and the shell desks again.

The classroom is a complete mess.

Nervously, I start to very slowly pull my tentacles back.

But not fast enough. Without any warning, every fin, shell, tail and scale start to turn toward me.

There's not a single sound - just a whole lot of blinking.

Visit BelowH2OBooks.com/fun_and_games
and enjoy free downloadable activities

Manufactured by Amazon.ca
Bolton, ON